THE WICKED BIG TODDLAH

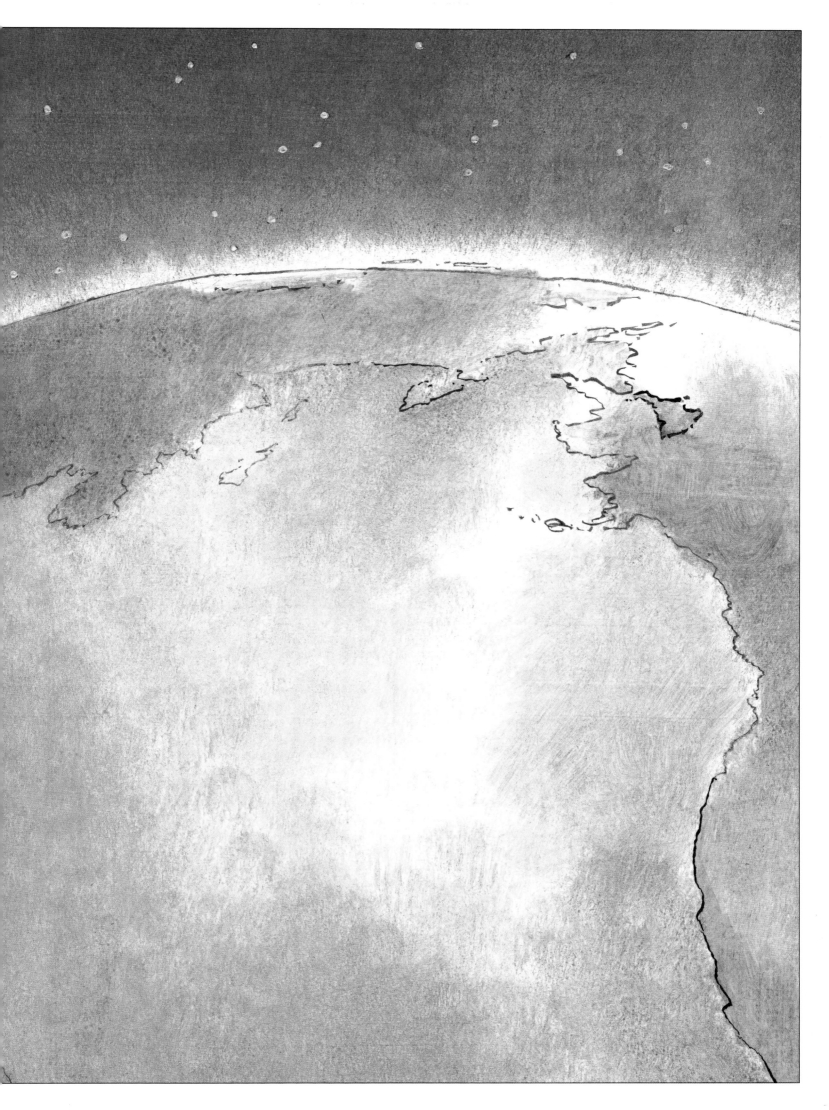

THE WICKED BIG TODDLAH

KEVIN HAWKES

DRAGONFLY BOOKS ———✦ NEW YORK

To the five toddlahs

All rights reserved. Published in the United States by Dragonfly Books,
an imprint of Random House Children's Books, a division of Random House, Inc., New York.
Originally published in hardcover in the United States by Alfred A. Knopf,
an imprint of Random House Children's Books, a division of Random House, Inc.,
New York, in 2007.

Dragonfly Books with the colophon is a registered trademark of Random House, Inc.

Visit us on the Web! www.randomhouse.com/kids

Educators and librarians, for a variety of teaching tools,
visit us at www.randomhouse.com/teachers

The Library of Congress has cataloged the hardcover edition of this work as follows:
Hawkes, Kevin.
The wicked big toddlah / Kevin Hawkes.
p. cm.
Summary: The first year in the life of a baby in Maine who is just like any other baby
except that he is gigantic.
ISBN 978-0-375-86188-8 (trade) — ISBN 978-0-375-96189-2 (lib. bdg.)
[1. Babies—Fiction. 2. Size—Fiction. 3. Maine—Fiction.] I. Title. II. Title: Wicked big toddler.
PZ7.H31324Wi 2007 [E]—dc22 2006032209

ISBN 978-0-440-41788-0 (pbk.)

MANUFACTURED IN CHINA

10 9 8 7 6 5 4

First Dragonfly Books Edition

The new baby came on the snowiest day of the year!

When my brothers and I went to visit him in
the hospital, he reached right out and grabbed
hold of my finger. Uncle Bert whistled, "That's
a wicked big toddlah ya got theyah, Jessie!"
So everybody called him Toddie from then on.

The next day, Toddie came home from
the hospital. I sat right next to him
and held his hand. He was wearin'
a new hat, mittens, and booties that
Mimmie Newcomb had knitted for him.
Every new baby gets a hat and booties
from Mimmie—it's a tradition!

It took Toddie a long time before he
could sleep through the whole night.
I played my fiddle to help calm him down.
Even the special cradle Uncle Bert and
Aunt Jo made for him didn't seem to help.

Takin' care of Toddie keeps everybody busy, especially when it's time to change the diaper. *Whew!*

Once Toddie learned to sit up,
taking baths was a lot of fun.
He loves to play with boats!

When Toddie's first tooth came in, he started eating SOLIDS! Uncle Bert and I even let him have ice cream. Mama wasn't too happy about that!

Toddie loves going camping.
He likes to splash his toes in
the lake and make his favorite
animal sounds. *Grrr*, says the
bear! *Snort*, says the moose!

When we go blueberry picking,
Toddie likes to eat more than he
picks. Babies are such messy eaters.

Raking leaves sure is fun with Toddie.
Now that he's crawling, it's harder to
keep track of him.

When all the relatives came at Thanksgiving time, Toddie was so excited that he said hello in his biggest Maine voice!

Toddie helped us put the lights up on
the barn at holiday time. And he took
his first steps!

On his first birthday,
Toddie got a special
birthday cake. He blew
out the candle all by himself,
which surprised everyone!

Toddie loves to be involved with everything—
even making maple syrup in the spring mud
season. He likes to take free samples now
and then.

"That's a wicked big mess!" says Uncle Bert.

Toddie's bedtime is Mama's favorite time of day.
We all sing Toddie to sleep while Uncle Bert
plays a soft lullaby. Once he's down for the
night, Toddie sleeps like a log . . .

. . . until it's wake-up time!